D1107591

HORACE D. LYON
NEW YORK CITY.

PIGS IS PIGS

# PIGS IS PIGS

*" Pets thim animals may be, an' domestic they be,
but pigs, I'm blame sure they do be "*

# PIGS IS PIGS

### BY

## ELLIS PARKER BUTLER

### Illustrations by Will Crawford

NEW YORK
McCLURE, PHILLIPS & CO.
MCMVI

Copyright, 1906, by McClure, Phillips & Co.

Published April, 1906

Fourth Impression.

Copyright, 1905, by Colver Publishing House
(American Magazine)

# LIST OF ILLUSTRATIONS

# PIGS IS PIGS

Mike Flannery, the Westcote agent of the Interurban Express Company, leaned over the counter of the express office and shook his fist. Mr. Morehouse, angry and red, stood on the other side of the counter, trembling with rage. The argument had been long and heated, and at last Mr. Morehouse had talked himself speechless. The cause of the trouble stood on the counter between the two men. It was a soap box across the top of which were nailed a number of strips, forming a rough but serviceable cage. In it two spotted guinea-pigs were greedily eating lettuce leaves.

"Do as you loike, then!" shouted Flannery, " pay for thim an' take thim, or don't pay for thim and leave thim be. Rules is rules, Misther Morehouse, an' Mike Flannery's not goin' to be called down fer breakin' of thim."

"But, you everlastingly stupid idiot!" shouted Mr. Morehouse, madly shaking a flimsy printed book beneath the agent's nose, "can't you read it here—in your own plain printed rates? 'Pets, domestic, Franklin to Westcote, if properly boxed, twenty-five cents each.'" He threw the book on the counter in disgust. "What more do you want? Aren't they pets? Aren't they domestic? Aren't they properly boxed? What?"

He turned and walked back and forth rapidly; frowning ferociously.

Suddenly he turned to Flannery, and forcing his voice to an artificial calmness spoke slowly but with intense sarcasm.

"Pets," he said "P-e-t-s! Twenty-five cents each. There are two of them. One! Two! Two times twenty-five are fifty! Can you understand that? I offer you fifty cents."

Flannery reached for the book.

He ran his hand through the pages and stopped at page sixty four.

"An' I don't take fifty cints," he whispered in mockery. "Here's the rule for ut. 'Whin the agint be in anny doubt regardin' which of two rates applies to a shipment, he shall charge the larger. The consign-ey may file a claim for the overcharge.' In this case, Misther Morehouse, I be in doubt. Pets thim animals may be, an' domestic they be, but pigs I'm blame sure they do be, an' me rules says plain as the nose on yer face, 'Pigs Franklin to Westcote, thirty cints each.' An' Mister Morehouse, by me arithmetical knowledge two

[ 6 ]

times thurty comes to sixty cints."

Mr. Morehouse shook his head savagely. "Nonsense!" he shouted, "confounded nonsense, I tell you! Why, you poor ignorant foreigner, that rule means common pigs, domestic pigs, not guinea-pigs!"

Flannery was stubborn.

"Pigs is pigs," he declared firmly. "Guinea-pigs, or dago pigs or Irish pigs is all the same to the Interurban Express Company an' to Mike Flannery. Th' nationality of the pig creates no differentiality in the rate, Misther Morehouse! 'Twould be the same was they Dutch pigs or Rooshun pigs. Mike Flannery," he added, "is here to tind to the expriss business and not to hould conversation wid dago pigs in sivinteen languages fer to discover be they Chinese or Tipperary by birth an' nativity."

Mr. Morehouse hesitated. He bit his lip and then flung out his arms wildly.

"Very well!" he shouted, "you shall hear of this! Your president shall hear of this! It is an outrage! I have offered you fifty cents. You refuse it! Keep the pigs until you are ready to take the fifty cents, but, by George, sir, if one hair of those pigs' heads is harmed I will have the law on you!"

He turned and stalked out, slamming the door. Flannery carefully lifted the soap box from the counter and placed it in a corner. He was not worried. He felt the peace that comes to a faithful servant who has done his duty and done it well.

Mr. Morehouse went home raging. His boy, who had been awaiting the guinea-pigs, knew better than to ask him for them. He was a normal boy and therefore always had a guilty conscience when his father was angry. So the boy slipped quietly around the house. There is nothing so soothing to a guilty conscience as to be out of the path of the avenger.

Mr. Morehouse stormed into the house. "Where's the ink?" he shouted at his wife as soon as his foot was across the doorsill.

Mrs. Morehouse jumped, guiltily. She never used ink. She had not seen the ink, nor moved the ink, nor thought of the ink, but her husband's tone convicted her of the guilt of having borne and reared a boy, and she knew that whenever her husband wanted anything in a loud voice the boy had been at it.

"I'll find Sammy," she said meekly.

When the ink was found Mr.

Morehouse wrote rapidly, and he read the completed letter and smiled a triumphant smile.

"That will settle that crazy Irishman!" he exclaimed. "When they get that letter he will hunt another job, all right!"

A week later Mr. Morehouse received a long official envelope with the card of the Interurban Express Company in the upper left corner. He tore it open eagerly and drew out a sheet of paper. At the top it bore the number A6754. The letter was short. "Subject—Rate on guinea-pigs," it said, "Dr. Sir—We are in receipt of your letter regarding rate on guinea-pigs between

Franklin and Westcote, addressed to the president of this company. All claims for overcharge should be addressed to the Claims Department."

Mr. Morehouse wrote to the Claims Department. He wrote six pages of choice sarcasm, vituperation and argument, and sent them to the Claims Department.

A few weeks later he received a reply from the Claims Department. Attached to it was his last letter.

"Dr. Sir," said the reply. "Your letter of the 16th inst., addressed to this Department, subject rate on guinea-pigs from Franklin to Westcote, rec'd. We have

[ 12 ]

taken up the matter with our agent at Westcote, and his reply is attached herewith. He informs us that you refused to receive the consignment or to pay the charges. You have therefore no claim against this company, and your letter regarding the proper rate on the consignment should be addressed to our Tariff Department."

Mr Morehouse wrote to the Tariff Department. He stated his case clearly, and gave his arguments in full, quoting a page or two from the encyclopedia to prove that guinea-pigs were not common pigs.

With the care that characterizes

corporations when they are systematically conducted, Mr. Morehouse's letter was numbered, O.K'd, and started through the regular channels. Duplicate copies of the bill of lading, manifest, Flannery's receipt for the package and several other pertinent papers were pinned to the letter, and they were passed to the head of the Tariff Department.

The head of the Tariff Department put his feet on his desk and yawned. He looked through the papers carelessly.

"Miss Kane," he said to his stenographer, "take this letter. 'Agent, Westcote, N. J. Please

[ 14 ]

advise why consignment referred to in attached papers was refused domestic pet rates.'"

Miss Kane made a series of curves and angles on her note book and waited with pencil poised. The head of the department looked at the papers again.

"Huh! guinea-pigs!" he said. "Probably starved to death by this time! Add this to that letter: 'Give condition of consignment at present.'"

He tossed the papers on to the stenographer's desk, took his feet from his own desk and went out to lunch.

When Mike Flannery received

the letter he scratched his head.

"Give prisint condition," he repeated thoughtfully. "Now what do thim clerks be wantin' to know, I wonder! 'Prisint condition,' is ut? Thim pigs, praise St. Patrick, do be in good health, so far as I know, but I niver was no veternairy surgeon to dago pigs. Mebby thim clerks wants me to call in the pig docther an' have their pulses took. Wan thing I do know, howiver, which is they've glorious appytites for pigs of their soize. Ate? They'd ate the brass padlocks off of a barn door! If the paddy pig, by the same token, ate as hearty as these dago pigs do, there'd be a famine in Ireland."

To assure himself that his report would be up to date, Flannery went to the rear of the office and looked into the cage. The pigs had been transferred to a larger box—a dry goods box.

"Wan,—two,—t'ree,—four,— foive, — six, — sivin, — eight!" he counted. "Sivin spotted an' wan all black. All well an' hearty an' all eatin' loike ragin' hippypotty-musses." He went back to his desk and wrote.

"Mr. Morgan, Head of Tariff Department," he wrote. " Why

do I say dago pigs is pigs because they is pigs and will be til you say they ain't which is what the rule book says stop your jollying me you know it as well as I do. As to health they are all well and hoping you are the same. P. S. There are eight now the family increased all good eaters. P. S. I paid out so far two dollars for cabbage which they like shall I put in bill for same what?"

Morgan, head of the Tariff Department, when he received this letter, laughed. He read it again and became serious.

"By George!" he said, "Flannery is right, 'pigs is pigs.' I'll

*" Flannery is right, pigs is pigs "*

have to get authority on this thing. Meanwhile, Miss Kane, take this letter: Agent, Westcote, N. J. Regarding shipment guinea-pigs, File No. A6754. Rule 83, General Instruction to Agents, clearly states that agents shall collect from consignee all costs of provender, etc., etc., required for live stock while in transit or storage. You will proceed to collect same from consignee."

Flannery received this letter next morning, and when he read it he grinned.

"Proceed to collect," he said softly. "How thim clerks do loike to be talkin'! *Me* proceed to collect two dollars and twinty-foive cints off Misther Morehouse! I wonder do thim clerks *know* Misther Morehouse? I'll git it! Oh, yes! 'Misther Morehouse, two an' a quarter, plaze.' 'Cert'nly, me dear frind F"annery. Delighted!' *Not!*"

Flannery drove the express wagon to Mr. Morehouse's door. Mr. Morehouse answered the bell.

"Ah, ha!" he cried as soon as he saw it was Flannery. "So you've come to your senses at last, have you? I thought you would! Bring the box in."

"I hev no box," said Flannery coldly. "I hev a bill agin Misther John C. Morehouse for two dollars

*" Proceed to collect "*

and twenty-foive cints for kebbages aten by his dago pigs. Wud you wish to pay ut?"

"Pay— Cabbages— !" gasped Mr. Morehouse. "Do you mean to say that two little guinea-pigs-"

"Eight!" said Flannery. "Papa an' mamma an' the six childer. Eight!"

For answer Mr. Morehouse slammed the door in Flannery's face. Flannery looked at the door reproachfully.

"I take ut the con-*sign*-y don't want to pay for thim kebbages," he said. "If I know signs of refusal, the con - *sign* - y refuses to pay for wan dang kebbage

[ 21 ]

leaf an' be hanged to me!"

Mr. Morgan, the head of the Tariff Department, consulted the president of the Interurban Express Company regarding guinea-pigs, as to whether they were pigs or not pigs. The president was inclined to treat the matter lightly.

"What is the rate on pigs and on pets?" he asked.

"Pigs thirty cents, pets twenty-five," said Morgan.

"Then of course guinea-pigs are pigs," said the president.

"Yes," agreed Morgan, "I look at it that way, too. A thing that can come under two rates is naturally due to be classed as the higher.

But are guinea-pigs, pigs? Aren't they rabbits?"

"Come to think of it," said the president, "I believe they are more like rabbits. Sort of half-way station between pig and rabbit. I think the question is this—are guinea-pigs of the domestic pig family? I'll ask professor Gordon. He is authority on such things. Leave the papers with me."

The president put the papers on his desk and wrote a letter to Professor Gordon. Unfortunately the Professor was in South America collecting zoological specimens, and the letter was forwarded to him by his wife. As the Professor was in

[ 23 ]

the highest Andes, where no white man had ever penetrated, the letter was many months in reaching him. The president forgot the guinea-pigs, Morgan forgot them, Mr. Morehouse forgot them, but Flannery did not. One-half of his time he gave to the duties of his agency; the other half was devoted to the guinea-pigs. Long before Professor Gordon received the president's letter Morgan received one from Flannery.

"About them dago pigs," it said, "what shall I do they are great in family life, no race suicide for them, there are thirty-two now shall I sell them do you take this express office for a menagerie, answer quick."

Morgan reached for a telegraph blank and wrote:

"Agent, Westcote. Don't sell pigs."

He then wrote Flannery a letter calling his attention to the fact that the pigs were not the property of the company but were merely being held during a settlement of a dispute regarding rates. He advised Flannery to take the best possible care of them.

Flannery, letter in hand, looked at the pigs and sighed. The dry-goods box cage had become too small. He boarded up twenty feet

[ 25 ]

of the rear of the express office to make a large and airy home for them, and went about his business. He worked with feverish intensity when out on his rounds, for the pigs required attention and took most of his time. Some months later, in desperation, he seized a sheet of paper and wrote "160" across it and mailed it to Morgan. Morgan returned it asking for explanation. Flannery replied:

"There be now one hundred sixty of them dago pigs, for heavens sake let me sell off some, do you want me to go crazy, what."

"Sell no pigs," Morgan wired.

Not long after this the president

of the express company received a letter from Professor Gordon. It was a long and scholarly letter, but the point was that the guinea-pig was the *Cavia aparoea* while the common pig was the genius *Sus* of the family *Suidae*. He remarked that they were prolific and multiplied rapidly.

"They are not pigs," said the president, decidedly, to Morgan. "The twenty-five cent rate applies."

Morgan made the proper notation on the papers that had accumulated in File A 6754, and turned them over to the Audit Department. The Audit Department took some time to look the matter up, and after the usual delay wrote Flannery that as he had on hand one hundred and sixty guinea-pigs, the property of consignee, he should deliver them and collect charges at the rate of twenty-five cents each.

Flannery spent a day herding his charges through a narrow opening in their cage so that he might count them.

"Audit Dept." he wrote, when he had finished the count, "you are way off there may be was one hundred and sixty dago pigs once, but wake up don't be a back number. I've got even eight hundred, now shall I collect for eight hundred or what, how about sixty-four dollars I paid out for cabbages.''

It required a great many letters back and forth before the Audit Department was able to understand why the error had been made of billing one hundred and sixty instead of eight hundred, and still more time for it to get the meaning of the '' cabbages.

Flannery was crowded into a few feet at the extreme front of the office. The pigs had all the rest of the room and two boys were employed constantly attending to them. The day after Flannery had counted the guinea-pigs there were eight more added to his drove, and by the time the Audit Department gave him authority to collect for eight hundred Flannery had given up all attempts to attend to the receipt or the delivery of goods. He was hastily building galleries around the express office, tier above tier. He had four thousand and sixty-four guinea-pigs to care for! More were arriving daily.

Immediately following its authorization the Audit Department sent another letter, but Flannery was too busy to open it. They wrote another and then they telegraphed:

"Error in guinea-pig bill. Collect for two guinea-pigs, fifty

*Mr. Morehouse had moved!*

cents. Deliver all to consignee."

Flannery read the telegram and cheered up. He wrote out a bill as rapidly as his pencil could travel over paper and ran all the way to the Morehouse home. At the gate he stopped suddenly. The house stared at him with vacant eyes. The windows were bare of curtains and he could see into the empty rooms. A sign on the porch said, "To Let." Mr. Morehouse had moved! Flannery ran all the way back to the express office. Sixty-nine guinea-pigs had been born during his absence. He ran out again and made feverish inquiries in the village. Mr. Morehouse had not only moved, but he had left West-cote. Flannery returned to the express office and found that two hundred and six guinea-pigs had entered the world since he left it. He wrote a telegram to the Audit Department.

"Can't collect fifty cents for two dago pigs consignee has left town address unkown what shall I do? Flannery."

The telegram was handed to one of the clerks in the Audit Department, and as he read it he laughed.

"Flannery must be crazy. He ought to know that the thing to do is to return the consignment here," said the clerk. He tele-

graphed Flannery to send the pigs
to the main office of the company
at Franklin.

When Flannery received the telegram he set to work. The six boys
he had engaged to help him also
set to work. They worked with
the haste of desperate men, making
cages out of soap boxes, cracker
boxes, and all kinds of boxes, and
as fast as the cages were completed
they filled them with guinea-pigs
and expressed them to Franklin.
Day after day the cages of guinea-
pigs flowed in a steady stream from
Westcote to Franklin, and still
Flannery and his six helpers ripped
and nailed and packed—relentlessly

and feverishly. At the end of the week they had shipped two hundred and eighty cases of guinea-pigs, and there were in the express office seven hundred and four more pigs than when they began packing them.

"Stop sending pigs. Warehouse full," came a telegram to Flannery. He stopped packing only long enough to wire back, "Can't stop," and kept on sending them. On the next train up from Franklin came one of the company's inspectors. He had instructions to stop the stream of guinea-pigs at all hazards. As his train drew up at Westcote station he saw a cattle-

*He was winding up the guinea-pig episode*

car standing on the express company's siding. When he reached the express office he saw the express wagon backed up to the door. Six boys were carrying bushel baskets full of guinea-pigs from the office and dumping them into the wagon. Inside the room Flannery, with his coat and vest off, was shoveling guinea-pigs into bushel baskets with a coal scoop. He was winding up the guinea-pig episode.

He looked up at the inspector with a snort of anger.

"Wan wagonload more an' I'll be quit of thim, an' niver will ye catch Flannery wid no more foreign pigs on his hands. No, sur! They near was the death o' me. Nixt toime I'll know that pigs of whativer nationality is domistic pets— an' go at the lowest rate."

He began shoveling again rapidly, speaking quickly between breaths.

"Rules may be rules, but you can't fool Mike Flannery twice wid the same thrick—whin ut comes to live stock, dang the rules. So long as Flannery runs this expriss office—pigs is pets—an' cows is pets—an' horses is pets—an' lions an' tigers an' Rocky Mountain goats is pets—an' the rate on thim is twinty - foive cints."

He paused long enough to let

one of the boys put an empty basket in the place of the one he had just filled. There were only a few guinea-pigs left. As he noted their limited number his natural habit of looking on the bright side returned.

"Well, annyhow," he said cheerfully, " 'tis not so bad as ut might be. What if thim dago pigs had been elephants!"

THE END